Pup Fiction™ Adventure Series

by

LaMonte Heflick

The Story of Fat Cat

The Story of Big Dog

The Story of Sweet the Skunk

The Story of Ninja Cat

The Story of Pup Daddy

The Story of Boney and Clyde

About the Author

LaMonte Heflick is a speech-language-hearing pathologist with the Elkhart Community Schools in Elkhart, Indiana. Mr. Heflick also teaches Chinese and Japanese at North Side, Pierre Moran, and West Side Middle Schools. In addition to his SLP license, Mr. Heflick is certified in Learning Disabilities, Teaching English to Speakers of Other Languages (TESOL), Japanese, and Mandarin Chinese.

The Story of Boney and Clyde

by LaMonte Heflick

Illustrated by John Lakey

Remedia Publications
Scottsdale, Arizona

Title: The Story of Boney and Clyde
ISBN# 1-56175-911-2

Published by:
Remedia Publications, Inc.
15887 N. 76th St. #120
Scottsdale, Arizona 85260
www.rempub.com

Cover Design by Don Merrifield

Boney

in Chicago, Illinois

She was a beautiful pup—a diamond in the rough.

Born on the wrong side of town. Life was hard.

Her mother got hit by a car. No brothers. No sisters.

Her father?

Nobody knows. Nobody knows.

PIZZ

She ran with the other dogs—street dogs. They came and went.

Hang out near a garbage dumpster behind a good restaurant and you can get by.

She got by.

But she was always thin. Too thin. That's why they called her Boney.

Clyde

He was not a cute, little doggy with a waggy tail.

He was tall. But not too tall. He was thin. But not skinny.

There was something about him that girl dogs liked.

He was fun. And girl dogs just want to have fun!

His name was Clyde.

He grew up in a tough neighborhood.

So he learned how to take care of himself.

His good looks helped. He had lots of friends.

They made him popular with the girl dogs, too.

Too popular. He liked the attention.

Some dogs say that's what got him into trouble—his need for attention.

South Bend

Boney was walking into the subway.

"Where you going, kid?" asked Max.

Boney turned towards the voice.

"Oh! Hi, Max," she said. "You scared me. I'm taking the train into South Bend. What's up with you?"

"Nothing much," said Max, grooming his whiskers.

"Nothing much?"

Boney put down her suitcase.

"I hear you're out on the streets. They say your old pal Al tossed you out."

"It was time to leave anyway, kitten."

Max put on a plastic smile.

"Street Cat, too?"

"Yeah," said Max. "Street Cat, too."

"What about Fuzz Ball?"

He’s Gone

“Fuzz Ball?” Max’s jaw dropped. “He’s gone. He got hit by a bus about a month ago.”

“Oh no!” said Boney. “Sorry to hear that.”

“Thanks, Boney.” Max looked down, then back up slowly. “I don’t want to keep you. You’ll miss your train.”

Boney smiled. “Take care, Max.”

She waved. “Maybe I’ll run into you when I get back into town.”

“So long.” He waved a paw as she turned to leave.

Boney picked up her bag. She was just a poor Chicago street dog, but Max couldn’t help thinking that she had class.

He watched her walk towards the trains. “Yes,” he said to himself as he rubbed his chin. “There goes a real fine lady.”

Boney climbed aboard the 5:00 p.m. train for Indiana.

COMICS
DOG

Eyes Meet

Sometimes things happen on a train. Eyes meet. Doors open.

Clyde was seated next to the window. He was reading a cheap comic book. He didn't look up, but he knew she was there.

His nose told him **all** that he needed to know. Unlike people, dogs depend on their sense of smell.

She, on the other paw, was showing some interest.

Who is this tall, dark stranger? she thought. *He looks to be not much more than a puppy but something is ... different.*

He's ***all*** *dog. I don't mean just another bag-of-bones* ***hound****. Maybe he's in the movies,* she thought. *He sure looks the part.*

Bow Wow

He didn't talk. He didn't need to.
He sat still and let his good looks do the work.

He continued to look at the comic book.

But he was no longer reading.
He just looked at the pictures.
Daydreaming.

The train left the station.

People relaxed into their seats. A family of cats took a nap.

An old raccoon talked endlessly to an even older squirrel who looked past him through pop-bottle glasses.

Clyde made his move.

"Excuse me," he said. "Do you have the time?"

Sorry

"What?" she asked, turning her head towards him.

He said it again, "Do you have the time?"

"I'm sorry. I must have been daydreaming."

She let out a long sigh as if she had been holding her breath.

"Yes, the time. Let's see ..." She looked at her watch. "It's 5:45."

"Thank you." He looked deep into her sky blue eyes. "My watch is in the shop," he said.

A long minute later he added, "Do you take the South Shore often?"

"No. This is only my second time. I'm going to visit my aunt in South Bend."

"South Bend? Not bad," he said. "I'm going into South Bend myself. I have a little ***banking business*** to take care of ... tomorrow morning."

Let Me Guess

"Let me guess," he said.

"You're a waitress. Your favorite color is blue. You're bored with your job. You would love to travel, but don't have the money."

"That's right. 100% correct," she smiled. "It's my turn," she said.

"You're a big-shot movie star. Your favorite color is red. You're doing a movie in California next week. And you came to Chicago on business."

"You're all wrong," he laughed. "I rob banks."

She looked shocked. Her eyes got big and her mouth fell open.

"You what?" she said.

Silence. Nobody said a word. Not one word.

You're Kidding

"You're just kidding," she said.

He shook his head. "Nope."

"This is some kind of a joke." She smiled.

"Nope." He took out his wallet and opened it. It was stuffed full of $5, $10, $20, and $50 bills.

"Well, Bow Wow," she said.

She ran her paw through her hair.

He put his wallet back in his pocket and leaned back in his seat.

The train rolled along the track.

Click, click. Click, click. Click, click.

After a long silence, she smiled.

"It sounds ... exciting, but dangerous."

The Train Rolled On

The train rolled on.

Boney looked out the window. She was thinking, *He looks so handsome. I thought he was a movie star. But he ain't. He's a bank robber. I won't say another word to him. I'll just mind my own business. But ... he's so good looking. And he's right about one thing—my job is boring. There ain't nothing exciting ever going to happen in my life. Nothing exciting at all.*

The train rolled on.

Clyde looked out the window. The sky was gray.

He was thinking, *I ain't no bank robber. What am I doing? Who am I trying to fool? I stole this money from my stepfather before I ran away. I ain't no big-shot movie star. And I ain't no big-time bank robber. But ... she thinks I* ***look*** *like one.*

Clyde smiled to himself. *She sure is pretty. She's probably from a poor family ... just like me. Yes, she sure is pretty. I bet she's part collie.*

Boney looked at him again—a quick glance. *I wonder how much money was in that fat wallet of his. He sure is a nice-looking dog; the nicest pup I've ever seen.*

The Train Rolled Down The Track

The cat family woke up. The kittens were hungry.

Momma cat took some rolls out of her purse. The kittens got quiet.

The squirrel tried his best to ignore the old raccoon.

The train rolled on down the track.

It made a brief stop near Michigan City.

NUTS

Clyde spoke, "When we get into South Bend, if you're not in too big of a hurry, maybe we could have dinner together."

"Tonight?" said Boney.

"Sure," said Clyde. "Why not?"

"Well ..." she thought a moment. "I guess that would be all right."

"Then it's a date," said Clyde.

Don't Look Too Interested

Clyde smiled. He picked up his comic book.

He was thinking again, *I don't want to look too interested. I'll just read my comic book. And keep an eye on her.*

Boney was thinking too, *What have I got to lose? When will I ever have another chance to meet another bank robber in my lifetime? He's so big and strong and handsome. The only dogs I ever meet are just that ...* ***dogs****. Dogs who drive trucks. Dogs who deliver bread. Dogs who howl all night.*

"Do you really, really, really rob banks?" she asked.

"I'm going to rob one first thing tomorrow morning," said Clyde.

Boney swallowed hard.

"Come along and watch me if you like," said Clyde.

Better Than Being A Waitress

It was more exciting than being a waitress.

Boney and Clyde walked into the Main Street Bank Tuesday morning at 9:00.

Clyde was scared to death.

He was thinking, *What am I doing? I ain't never robbed no bank before.*

Boney wasn't scared, she was excited.

She was thinking, *This is a lot more fun than being a waitress.*

"Okay," said Clyde. "Now everybody just listen to me and you won't get hurt. This is a bank robbery. I'm Clyde Marrow. And this here is Boney Barker."

Silence. Nobody said a word. Not one sound.

"Now ... open that drawer and empty it out into this bag."

The Cops

The police siren was loud. It was real loud. RRRRRRRRRRRRRRR!

Boney could feel her heart beating like a drum.

She was first out the door.

Clyde was right on her heels.

A cop dog on foot was running towards the bank from the south. And a cop dog van was coming up the street from the north.

"Quick!" shouted Clyde, as he signaled Boney.

"This way! Down the alley!"

Boney tripped. Clyde helped her up.

The cop dog, a spotted fox terrier, was young and fast.

Boney and Clyde were young, too. And they were faster.

Arf! Arf!

"Arf! Arf! Arf!" The cop dogs ran into the alley.

"Bow Wow! Bow Wow! Bow Wow!"

They chased Boney and Clyde, barking loudly at their heels.

"This way!" yelled Clyde. "This way. Faster!"

Of all things, Boney was laughing, but she was running as fast as her skinny legs would carry her.

They ducked into a doorway.

Then they ran down a long hall.

They tried a door. No luck, it was locked.

They tried another door, it was open.

Clyde slammed it hard behind them.

They were both breathing hard.

"Listen."

"Arf! Arf! Arf!" They could hear the cop dogs.

Grrrrrrrrr

The cop dogs were fooled, but only for a minute.

Cop dogs are known for their keen sense of smell.

And Clyde knew it.

"Quick, Boney," he whispered.

"The window, over there ... it's open."

Outside the door they could hear the cop dogs: "Grrrrrrrrrrrrrr ..."

They held paws.

They ran towards the window.
Without looking, they jumped.

They landed in a trash dumpster.

"Garbage!"

Soft, wet, stinky garbage.

"Yuck!"

"At least we didn't break our necks," said Clyde.

Criminals

They had robbed a bank.

They had slipped through the paws of the cops.

But they were criminals now. And they could be identified.

The people, the dogs, the cats in the bank had seen their faces.

The tough cop dogs would be on the lookout.

CHECK OUT TIME

They hurried to the outskirts of town and checked into a cheap hotel under the name of Mr. and Mrs. Bones.

They took a room on the 3rd floor, away from the street.

"Clyde," whispered Boney. "How much money did we get?"

"Let's take a look," said Clyde.

Lay Low

They counted the loot together. "$15,438."

"That's a lot of money!" howled Boney.

"That's right," said Clyde.

"Well, let's go out to a fancy restaurant and live it up!" Boney said with a big smile.

"We can't," said Clyde. "At least not right away.

We have to lay low for a few weeks ... maybe longer."

"A few weeks ... maybe longer?" groaned Boney.

"That's right," said Clyde.

"You mean we have to stay here in this dump?"

"That's right. You got it. Sorry."

We Need Your Wheels

"This place stinks, and we have enough money to buy a castle."

Clyde walked to the window and looked out.

He didn't take the time to count, but there were at least 4 or 5 squad cars out front.

"Quick, Boney! Out the back way! Hurry!"

Clyde pushed the door open, knocking a cop dog down.

"Look out, Clyde!" screamed Boney.

Two more cop dogs were just getting off the elevator.

"Out the fire escape, Boney. Fast! Come on, come on!"

Clyde ran into the street.

An old cat in a Ford truck hit the brakes.

Clyde opened the door and pulled the surprised driver out. "Slide out, buddy! We need your wheels!" he shouted. "Get in, Boney!"

The Getaway

Clyde put the pedal to the floor.

The old Ford spit smoke. The tires spun. The truck fish-tailed until the rubber finally gripped the pavement.

The cop dogs scrambled into their cars. Engines roared.

The chase was on.

40, 50, 55, 60 mph ... Clyde raced through the streets.

The cop dogs were experienced drivers.

And their cars were fast.

The chase continued.

Boney was scared now. This was *more than excitement.* There was nothing fun or funny about it.

She turned around to see the cop dogs closing in.

Clyde sped around a corner. He turned sharp. Too sharp. The old truck lifted up on 2 wheels.

The Radio

Red Dog was in the first car behind Clyde.

He was on the radio. "All cars, all cars ... the getaway truck is on Michigan Street near the river. Let's box them in."

Up ahead Clyde could see it. The cops had set up a road block. He hit the brakes hard. *Screech!*

He shifted into reverse. Looking over his right shoulder, he backed down the middle of the street.

Crash! He smashed into the front of Red Dog's squad car.

"All right! Get out slowly with your paws up!" yelled Captain Brown Rusty.

"We've got to make a run for it," said Boney.

"No, Boney," Clyde begged. "No, no, no ..."

But it was too late. Boney threw her door open and ran up the street.

Look Out!

"Arf! Arf! Arf!" A cop dog chased after her.

"Hold it right there," barked another cop.

"Look out!" screamed a woman on the sidewalk.

The cop dog in the squad car coming in fast from West Street didn't have time to stop.

There was nothing he could do. It was too late.

Boney lay on the street.

A crowd of people, dogs, and cats gathered around.

She didn't move.

The cops let Clyde see her.

They gave him a few minutes to say good-bye before they put her into the ambulance.

Crime Doesn't Pay

"Crime doesn't pay," said Brown Rusty as he put a paw on Clyde's shoulder.

Clyde was silent.

After a long minute ... "Okay, son," said Rusty. "Let's go."

Clyde got into the back seat of the cop car.

People came close to have a look.

"Look," said one woman. "That's Clyde Marrow, the bank robber."

Another woman said, "That's the dog I saw running from the bank."

Clyde didn't even notice them.

He was silent.

He always liked attention. He loved it. He lived for it. But not like this. No, not like this.

The Newspaper

The newspaper headlines the next day read: NO MORE BARK LEFT IN BONEY AND CLYDE.

The courtroom was full.

Clyde sat still as the judge entered.

"All rise. The court of Judge Milton Canine is now in session."

The judge spoke softly, "The jury has found you guilty, Clyde Morrow. It is my duty to pronounce your sentence: You will go to the state penetentiary at Michigan City for a period of no less than six years."

Clyde stared at the floor. He didn't move. It was real to him now. It was over.

The Letter

On his first night in jail, Clyde wrote a letter to Boney's aunt in South Bend, Indiana.

The letter said:

Dear Mollie Barker,

I'm sorry for what has happened.

I'm sorry for all the pain that I have caused you.

I have done wrong. I know it.

And I will have to live with it for the rest of my life. If there was anything that I could do to bring back Boney I would do it.

But it's over.

And I'm sorry. Please forgive me.

Respectfully,

Clyde Marrow